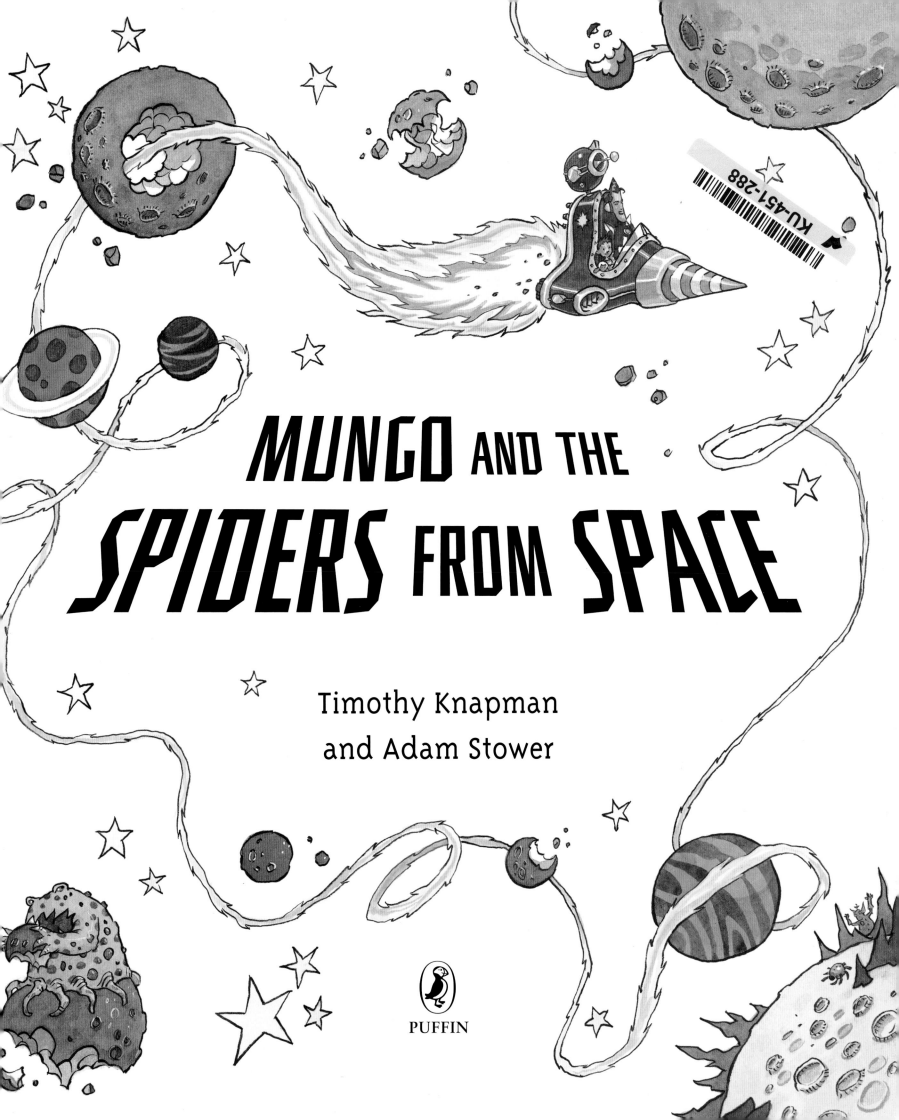

MUNGO AND THE
SPIDERS FROM SPACE

Timothy Knapman
and Adam Stower

PUFFIN

This is Mungo.
Mungo's just been given a book called
GALACTICUS AND GIZMO SAVE THE UNIVERSE!

His mum found it at a jumble sale.
It was old and torn and tatty and stuck together
with sticky tape, but she knew Mungo would
love it, just from the picture on the cover.

"Read it, Mum!
Read it, PLEASE!"
said Mungo that night.

AND THIS IS THE STORY IT TELLS...

GALACTICUS and GIZMO

SAVE THE UNIVERSE!

The trusty rocket ship **Vroom-101** streaked across the winking, blinking blackness of space. AT THE CONTROLS: **Captain Galacticus of Star Squadron** and his sparky sidekick, **Gizmo.**

They were taking the **GNASHING, SLASHING GOBBLEBEAST** to space prison for eating two galaxies and a Mars.

OUR STORY SO FAR:

CEASE AND DESIST!

CEASE AND DESIST!

WHEN SUDDENLY . . .

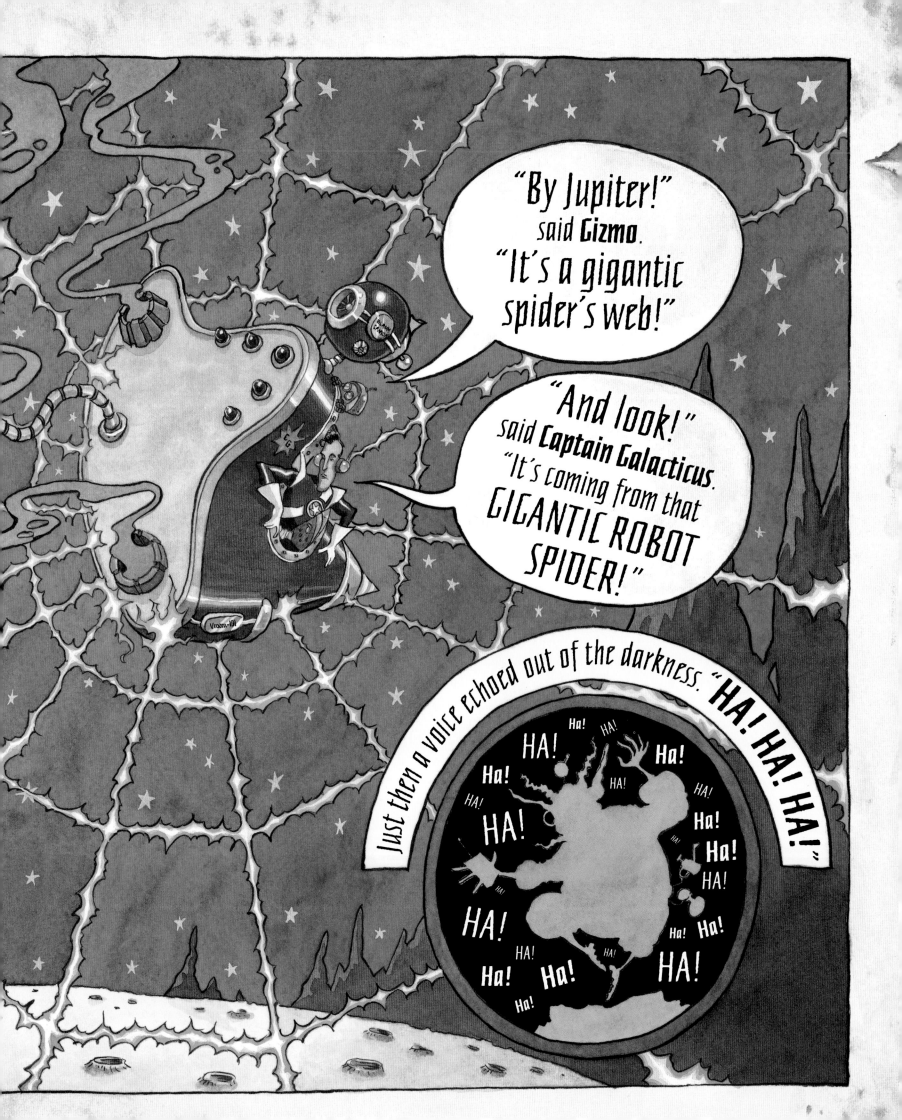

"I'd know that crazed cackle anywhere!"
said **Captain Galacticus.**

"It's **Dr Frankenstinker** –
the maddest mad scientist on Mercury!"

Wicked Dr Frankenstinker!

Who rearranged the stars so they'd
spell out rude words!

Wild Dr Frankenstinker!

Who squeezed all the milk out of
the Milky Way just so he could
have it on his cornflakes!

Weird Dr Frankenstinker!

Whose shocking behaviour was
blamed on a nasty case of asteroids
he'd had when he was small.

"We meet again at last, Galacticus!"
said **Dr Frankenstinker**. "But you won't stop me this time.
Soon every Star Squadron rocket ship will be tangled up in a web like
this one – and then I will rule the universe! **HA! HA! HA!**"

"NOT SO FAST,"
said **Dr Frankenstinker**.
"My spider army and I are off to defeat Star Squadron, but, don't worry, we won't be leaving you all alone and sad."

"In fact, you'll be tickled pink!"

"SEIZE HIM!"

The next thing he knew, **Captain Galacticus** was once again held fast in a GIGANTIC SPIDER'S WEB!

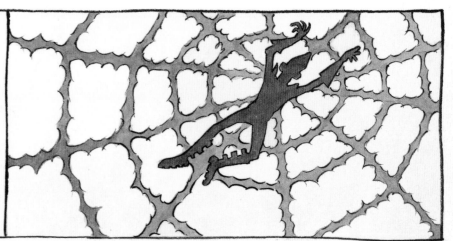

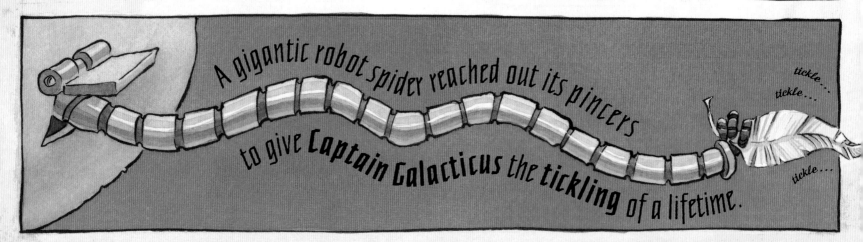

A gigantic robot spider reached out its pincers to give **Captain Galacticus** the **tickling** of a lifetime.

tickle...
tickle...
tickle...

"Ooh, no! Ha! Ha! Please! Tee hee! HELP! HELP!!" he yelped.

WOULD GIZMO HEAR THE CAPTAIN'S YELP FOR HELP?
WOULD SHE RESCUE HIM IN TIME?
WOULD THEY BE ABLE TO FOIL DR FRANKENSTINKER'S
DASTARDLY PLAN TO RULE THE UNIVERSE?

Mungo couldn't wait to find out. But . . .

THE
LAST PAGE
WAS
MISSING!

"But, Mum!" said Mungo.
"What happens next?"
"I don't know, darling,"
she said. "Why don't you
make up an ending?"
And she left him alone
with the book.

Make up an ending?
thought Mungo. I can't
make up an ending!

And then something
odd happened.

As he sat staring
at the cover, one
of the stars . . .

started to get bigger.

And bigger.

And bigger.

UNTIL . . .

With a

BOOM!

and a

Zoom!

The rocket ship,
Vroom-IOI
burst into the room.
"By Jupiter!"
said Mungo.

Before he knew what was happening, it scooped him up . . .

and looped the loop and swooped straight back into the book!

Wooosshh . . .

"But that's cheating!" said **Mungo**. "I've got to do SOMETHING!"

"BUT WHAT BUTTON DO I PRESS?"

Mungo couldn't decide – so he shut his eyes and pressed them ALL.

Whizz-up!

Zwip!

sproing!

Cring!

Fwee!

The rocket ship went STREAKING and SHRIEKING . . .

and *poinked* Dr Frankenstinker IN THE **BOTTOM**.

"YEE-OUCH!" he yelped and he BLERPED back the page.
"GRAB IT!" said Gizmo.
"UGH!" said Captain Galacticus. "It's all soggy!"

When Mungo's mum came back to turn off the light, Mungo was fast asleep. He was still clutching the last page of the book in which Captain Galacticus was rescued and the universe was saved by a mysterious stranger . . .

... the youngest ever member of Star Squadron.

To James and Rowan, heroes of Star Squadron, with love – T.K.

For Matt and Anne, with love – A.S.

PUFFIN BOOKS

Published by the Penguin Group: London, New York, Australia,
Canada, India, Ireland, New Zealand and South Africa
Penguin Books Ltd, Registered Offices: 80 Strand, London WC2R 0RL, England

puffinbooks.com

First published 2007
3 5 7 9 10 8 6 4 2
Text copyright © Timothy Knapman, 2007
Illustrations copyright © Adam Stower, 2007
Made and printed in China
ISBN: 978–0–141–50056–0